IAN, CEO, NORTH POLE

IAN, CEO, NORTH POLE

By

Eric Dana Hansen

Eloquent Books
New York, New York

Eloquent Books
An imprint of AEG Publishing Group
845 Third Avenue, 6th Floor - 6016
New York, NY 10022
www.eloquentbooks.com

ISBN: 978-1-60693-554-5 1-60693-554-2

Printed in the United States of America

Book Design: SP

Table Of Contents

Chapter One

Ian was having problems at work. He had been with Santa for a couple of years and he'd held different jobs in Santa's toy factory, but none of them seemed right for him. He wasn't sure why. Actually, Ian didn't work in the toy factory itself. He worked in the warehouse next door, where the toys were stored until Santa delivered them on Christmas Eve.

He remembered when he was an apprentice; one of his first jobs was to help pack the toys. He got to hold the peanut dispenser and point it at the open boxes. He liked to watch the peanuts flow out of the nozzle because they reminded him of snowflakes that turned into snowballs.

Ian would dream about playing in the snow and having a snowball fight with the other elves. Then they would build little igloos and hide from each other. Sometimes they would just take naps in the igloos and dream about all sorts of things. Ian often dreamt about traveling around the world and playing with other kids. He would go….

"Ian!" a voice screeched from the loudspeaker. "Turn that thing off! You're getting peanuts all over the place!"

Ian was startled out of his daydream and looked around. All of his fellow elves were laughing. They could always count on Ian for a good laugh. Ian hung his head and apologized.

His boss, Cedric, sighed and thought "What am I going to do with Ian? He's such a good-hearted elf and a good worker, but he day dreams too much. I'd better see about getting him a different job." Cedric decided to talk to Santa.

He was able to meet with Santa at the end of the day.

"Santa," said Cedric. "I've got a bit of a problem in the packing department. One of my elves, Ian is his name, can't seem to keep his mind on his work. He daydreams a lot. He's basically a good elf, but I don't think he fits this job. Do you think we can move him to another job?"

Santa stroked his white beard and listened carefully.

"Hmm," he muttered. "I know Ian, and I know what you're saying. I believe that he means well and he's a quick learner. Maybe we should move him over to the Picking Department. He could pick out the toys from the warehouse shelves and deliver them to the packers. Shall we try that?"

Cedric took off his cap and scratched his head.

"Yeah, Santa, that could work. Over there in picking, he'll have to move pretty fast and maybe he won't have time to day dream. Let's give it a try."

So, the next day, Ian reported to Picking. He liked the idea of a change because he thought the packing job was somewhat boring.

"That's probably why I was always day-dreaming," he told himself. Over the next few days, he learned how to be a picker.

It was pretty easy. They gave him a list with the kids' names, their addresses, and the toys they had asked for. Santa had already checked the list twice to see if the kids had been naughty or nice so he didn't have to worry about that. Then he went into the warehouse and looked for the toys.

The toys were pretty easy to find because they were stored alphabetically. For instance, on the "A" shelf you would find alligator puppets or airplanes, on "B" would be basketballs and books, and on "C" car toys or cradles for baby dolls and so on.

Ian liked to see how fast he could find something. He pushed himself very hard and soon found that he could find most everything really fast. He was happy and proud.

After he found the different toys, he would put a tag on them and deliver them to the packers. He would then make an entry in the book to show that every toy for every child had been found and delivered for packing. Ian liked this part of the job.

It was amazing how many different names there were in the world. Names for kids and names for places where they lived. He tried to guess what the different places were like, what the kids did, what they ate, or what school was like. Since Ian could find things so fast, he had lots of time left over. One day, he found a computer in the warehouse that wasn't being used. He did searches on the Internet to find out more about the different countries and their people. It was all really interesting. He would imagine himself traveling to visit these kids in different countries. They played games and then had Christmas dinner with their families. It was so cool!

Ian saw himself in a dining room with a huge table full of all kinds of delicious food. There were many people in the room. They were from all over the world and they were having a wonderful Christmas feast. He found that he could eat as much as he wanted and then he could even have seconds of dessert! He was reaching for another bowl of ice cream with chocolate syrup and a cherry on top.....

"Ian!" barked the loudspeaker. "Where are you? You're holding things up! Report to my desk, immediately!"

"Oh, oh," thought Ian. "That was Gabriel, my boss. Not as easy going as Cedric was. I'd better get a move on." He ran back to his work station and reported to Gabriel. "I'm sorry sir. I was doing some extra research so I'd know more about the kids that will receive these presents. I thought that if I knew more about them, I could be more efficient."

"You've got to be kidding," shouted Gabriel. "You're just supposed to put the tags on the toys and put a note in the book. Then deliver them to the packers. No more!" Do you understand?"

"Yes sir, I understand," muttered Ian as he returned to his bench.

The other elves tried not to laugh but it was a challenge.

Ian pushed himself again and soon set new speed records in finding toys and putting the address tags on them. Pretty soon the packer elves couldn't keep up with him and they started to get mad. Many of them wouldn't talk to him and it hurt him. He also missed doing the background research about the different lands and different people. He was starting to feel very confused again. He decided to call Samuel.

Samuel and he had been best friends almost since they were born. They spent most of their spare time together, playing, reading, or just hanging out and talking. They had worked together in packing until Ian was moved. Samuel liked working in packing and he got along well with the other elves. He was kind of like their unofficial leader.

Ian called Samuel on his cell phone. "Hey, Samuel, how's it going?"

"Everything's going well, Ian," Samuel responded. "How about

12

you?"

"Oh, I don't know," said Ian. "Some of the guys aren't talking to me and I thought maybe you were behind schedule or something."

"No, not at all," said Samuel. "Actually, you've made us look good because you're so fast. What they're mad about is that sometimes you're too fast. Then it makes us look slow. Doesn't bother me, but it sure does bother some of them. I told then to chill out, but you know how that goes."

"You know, Samuel, before, when I got ahead, I used to get on the computer and do research on the kids that were going to receive the presents. You know, because I had the time," said Ian. "But, one day, I forgot the time and caused the pickers to get behind and Gabriel didn't like it at all. He said that he didn't want me to do research anymore. I was just supposed to concentrate on picking. What do you think?"

Without hesitating, Samuel responded. "I think you ought to move again."

"But I just got here!" Ian replied with a look of despair.

"I know" said Samuel. "But it's obviously not the job for you. Better to move now before you cause all kinds of problems for yourself and everyone else. Don't you think that makes sense?"

"Yeah, I guess you're right," said Ian. "But what do you think I should do?" he asked with a voice full of despair.

"Why don't you try shipping?" suggested Samuel. "They're the last stop before Santa takes off. They have to do research about the different lands. You know, so they can provide Santa with a map and other information, too. Information like what's going on in different places around the world. He needs this info so he doesn't waste time while he's making his deliveries. Since you like to do research on the Internet, I think you'll find this job to be right up your alley. Don't you?"

"You know, Samuel," Ian responded. "You might have something there. I'll talk to my boss and see what he thinks. Maybe we can work something out. Thanks a lot for listening to me. You're a great friend, but don't let it go to your head," he laughed. "I'll talk to you later," and they hung up.

Chapter Two

Ian felt much better as he headed for Gabriel's office.

"I hope he'll listen to me," he muttered to himself.

"Come in," yelled Gabriel in what Ian hoped was a friendly tone. "What can I do for you?" he asked.

"Sir," I'd like to talk about how I've been doing. Is that okay?"

"Well, you know we have our regular appraisals after 90 days on the job," said Gabriel. "You've only been on the job a month," he added. What's the hurry?"

"Well, I know that picking is important," Ian began. "But, when I first took this job, I thought that there would be a chance to do some research on where the presents go, you know, what the kids are like in different countries, what their families are like, how they celebrate Christmas, what kind of food they eat, and so forth. But I found out that this is really part of the shipping job. Do you think maybe I could move over there?" he asked.

Gabriel's eyes rolled back as he pushed himself away from his desk. "This guy Ian is driving me nuts," he thought to himself. "Thank heaven Santa is a good guy and wants to keep his elves happy, (and busy). He always says, *"A busy Elf is a happy Elf."* I guess he should know what he's talking about after all this time. I'll give Arvid a call," he muttered to himself as he stood up.

"Ian", he said. "I'm going to talk to Arvid. He's in charge of shipping. If he says okay, well, then we can talk to Santa. I'm hoping he'll go along with us. We'll get back to you in a day or two."

Ian sighed with relief as he walked out of Gabriel's office. He later called Samuel and gave him an update. Samuel said that it sounded good. All Ian had to do now was wait.

After what seemed like an eternity, Ian got a call from Gabriel.

"Arvid said it would be okay," Gabriel began. "He said he had another guy that we can trade for you so I don't run short in picking, and Santa gave us his blessing. So you can start over there tomorrow and good luck to you. I hope that you find what you're looking for."

Ian practically exploded with pent-up tension and excitement. He couldn't wait to start his new job in shipping. But first, of course, he had to brag to Samuel. And, of course, Samuel was happy for him. What a great buddy!

Before going to bed, Ian read the job description for the shipping department.

Receive packages from packing dept.
Read label and make sure the name and address can be easily read.
Enter the name and address into the computer.
Computer provides details about the local culture for that address:
Are the roofs flat or peaked?
How big are the chimneys?
What kind of food treats should Santa expect?

Check the correct pronunciation of the family names, (in case Santa runs into one of the parents);
Any special news about the family?
Any special information about the children?

Ian's head was swimming as he dropped off to sleep.

The next morning, Ian reported to Arvid, his new boss. Arvid took him on a tour and introduced him to the other elves that worked in shipping. After that, they sat down in Arvid's office and reviewed the responsibilities of the shipping job.

"This is one of the most important jobs in Santa's entire domain," Arvid began. "We have some simple rules here," he continued. "Rule #1 is to *obey all rules*. Rule #2 is to *never assume anything*. You have to know and understand everything completely, so Santa always has the right information."

Arvid caught his breath and continued, "Santa needs to know where he's going at all times. He's never once been lost, although he had a close call with fog one time. Fortunately, Rudolph saved the day, or night, so to speak. Well, I guess that's it," he concluded. "Any questions?"

Ian was excited. Maybe kind of scared, too. This was an important job. He'd better do his homework!

"Will I be able to find all my answers on the Internet?" he asked.

"For the most part, yes," Arvid responded. "But I encourage you to ask your co-workers, too," he added. "They have many years of experience and lots of knowledge. They can often get you an answer faster than you can on your own, so don't hesitate to ask them, okay? Any other questions?"

There were none, so they ended their meeting.

With that, Ian went out to his designated work space and started on his first package. It was addressed to a boy named Hans Peter who lived in a little village on the Isle of Fyn in Denmark. The village was called Aebleby. Ian couldn't wait to get on the computer. "I wonder what it's like in Aebleby?" he thought.

Ian remembered what Arvid had said about asking his co-workers and so he did.

"Can you tell me anything about Aebleby?' Ian asked an elf named Kai that worked across from him.

"Sure can," said Kai. "Aebleby is about 15 to 20 kilometers southwest of the port city of Nyborg," he continued. "Santa is very familiar with that part of Denmark and he knows about Hans Peter, too. Hey, I'll bet that's a bow and arrow you've got in that box there, isn't it?"

"Yeah, it is," Ian said with a questioning look. "But how did you know?"

"Well, I remember last year there was another boy in Aebleby named Kresten who asked for a bow and arrow," Kai began. "Kresten was about a year older than Hans Peter and Santa had a feeling that Hans Peter would ask for one this year since they lived so close and played together all the time, I'll bet you've heard the expression, *It's a Small World,* haven't you? Well, we see examples of that all the time, here at the North Pole," he added. "In fact, we kind of help Santa make the world smaller."

Ian nodded his head in agreement, (and amazement!) "This is so cool!" he thought.

"So, Santa doesn't really need much help with this delivery to Hans Peter, does he?" asked Ian, as he held up the bow and arrow box.

"No, I don't think so. He knows that part of the country and the people pretty well because they're so close to the North Pole," answered Kai. "But there's been a lot of migration of people around the world," he continued. "Including Denmark. Santa needs a lot of help locating kids in their new homes. It can be very complicated at times. That's why we're here," he beamed!

Ian couldn't have been more pleased with his new assignment. This was important! Santa really needed lots of support to find everybody and deliver everything on Christmas Eve.

Ian thought again about Rudolph, the red-nosed reindeer and how, at one time, he had come out of almost nowhere to rescue Santa and the other reindeer on Christmas Eve. "I wonder what would have happened if Rudolph hadn't shown up?" he thought to himself.

Chapter Three

At his job orientation, Arvid had explained to Ian that he would need to do some background research on Santa Claus. He needed to learn things about his history, how different people and cultures around the world celebrate Christmas and so on. Arvid encouraged him to do this research when things were slow at work or on his days off. This was not a problem for Ian because he enjoyed doing searches on the Internet and had a computer at home. He was ready to go!

One thing Ian never understood was why Santa Claus would choose the North Pole, with its freezing temperatures all year long, for his home and workshops. Ian's first search produced the following answer, *"Just remember that Santa Claus belongs to the world -- to any country -- so the top of the world, which is not owned by any one country, is the perfect spot."* Ian liked this answer!

Another question Ian had was, 'how old is Santa Claus'? Well, he couldn't find out for sure on the Internet and none of his fellow elves knew either, but he did find the following:

"Santa's village is approximately 1,700 years old. How old is

Santa? Well, he has been around a long time and obviously benefits from living in the bitter cold of the North Pole. Santa prefers to think of age as a state of mind, rather than a real number."

This was good enough for Ian!

What about himself and the other elves? How long had they been around? Ian had never talked about this with anybody. He didn't remember anyone else that ever discussed themselves. He had discovered some information, though.

Elves: Where did they come from? How did they come to be? No one really knows for sure. Suffice it to say that Santa's elves are fantastic workers. Their only goal in life is to work hard and make sure the Christmas mission is a success.

Some elves are three to four feet tall. Others, like Ian, are much taller, in fact, almost the same height as humans. Some elves have pointed ears, others don't. Ian didn't, but he never thought much about that, one way or another. To him, ears were simply for listening and he could hear fine!

Elves have different skin colors, just like the different people around the world. They can speak and understand any language. They love to eat and they love to try new recipes from different cultures! "Bring them on!" Ian muttered to himself with a big smile on his face.

Contrary to popular opinion, not all elves have the same skills. Some are good toy makers, while others are better working with the reindeer. Some are more geared toward technology, so they handle the databases (including the "naughty and nice" list). Others prefer to work at maintaining and building new workshops in Santa's village. Some are groomed to be leaders.

Ian thought he was more technology oriented, but then he liked to do other things as well. He liked variety, which caused him some problems at times. He wasn't sure whether he'd be a good leader. He'd worry about that later. He was very happy in his shipping job so far, and he loved doing this research! Shipping was really cool! They even provided background music for the workers!

"We do our best to serve the rest
Of boys and girls in different worlds
Who celebrate a Christmas date
That's mostly in December.

We make the toys for girls and boys
Getting them ready feels so heady
We work all year round with heads to the ground
It really picks up in September

What Santa likes are toys and bikes
And dolls and cars or pink guitars
Over the years with yells and cheers
He gives kids lots to remember

What boys and girls like to do Christmas night
Is go to bed early and sleep really tight
Get up in the morning with parents still yawning
Take a peek in their stockings, so tender.

"Santa was here!" A kid shouts with cheer.
"He knew I was good!" (And his folks understood)
"Santa," he said, "has a really good head"
"He remembered my toy, what a memory!"

Ian really loved this song. The Elves in shipping had written it years ago and they sang it often, especially when they really started to get busy toward year end. He whistled as he headed home after work. He was really looking forward to doing lots of Internet searches about Christmas around the world.

Chapter 4

"Hey Kai," Ian said as he started work the next morning. "I've got to do this background research on how Christmas is celebrated around the world. You know what I'm talking about? I'm kind of looking forward to it, but I'll tell you one thing for sure, I have no clue where to begin. Any thoughts?" he asked.

"Yeah, I know what you mean," Kai answered. "When I was new to the group like you, I developed a study plan. What I did was start at the top of the world and then kind of zigzagged up and down with the time zones, you know, the way Santa does. It seemed kind of logical and it really helped me stay organized," he said. "Get yourself a globe and chart a path. It'll give you a feel for how Santa navigates too and that's really cool," he added.

"Great idea," Ian answered. "I'm going to give it a try. Thanks!"

"There's another option that might work for you, too," Kai added. "A support group was formed a few years ago that helps guys like yourself, you know, new on the job and the like. They get together to discuss the different cultural things that they discover. You know, to kind of put some sense to everything. I joined it when I was new and it was the best thing that could have happened to me."

"Sounds interesting!" Ian answered. "Where can I find out some more about it?"

"Call Mrs. Claus' receptionist," Kai offered. "Tell her that you're interested in the **Cultural Studies Support Group**. She'll hook you up with someone from the group."

Ian called Samuel that night.

"Hey Samuel, have you ever heard about the Cultural Studies Support Group?" he asked.

"Yeah, I've heard about it," Samuel answered. "But I never joined it," he added. "Sometimes I wish that I had, but I was just too busy with other stuff at the time. Besides, I'm kind of bashful and I heard that you had to give speeches about what you were learning and this kind of turned me off," he added finishing in a whisper.

"Gosh, I'm kind of that way too. Do you think I'd fit in?" Ian asked.

"Well, if you don't like it, you can always quit," Samuel offered.

"Yeah, I guess I could," Ian said with a catch in his voice. "Maybe I'll give them a call," he gulped.

The next day at work, he knew he should call the receptionist, but kept putting it off. Finally, at home, he sat there with his finger on the dial pad for a long time. When he finally did dial the number he got a recording, "This is Mrs. Claus' office. I'm sorry we missed your call. Our office hours are 8 AM to 5 PM. If this is an emergency, please dial "0". Well, Ian didn't think this was an emergency so he decided he'd call in the morning when he was on break.

He slept fitfully that night, tossing and turning, thinking about making speeches and making a fool of himself and the other elves laughing.

The next day, during his morning break, he called the receptionist. He had a hard time getting it out. "I'm er, that is, I would like to uh, talk to somebody about the uh, Cultural Studies Support Group," he stuttered.

"And who am I talking to?" asked the receptionist in a professional tone.

"Uh, this is Ian. I just started working in the shipping department and I heard about this group," he said. "I've got a lot of research to do and this group can, uh, well, you know, it might be able to help me out?" he asked.

"Yes, it can," the receptionist answered. "The group varies in size from twelve to twenty elves and they help each other by sharing their research," she added.

"And, uh, how do they, uh, how do they," (arghh, he couldn't get the question out), that is, how do they, uh, do they share?" he finally blurted out.

"Why they just simply present their findings to the group," said the receptionist. "It's no big deal. Just a simple presentation."

"You mean like, a presentation that's kind of like a, you know, speech?" he shuddered.

"Exactly, she said. "No big deal."

Ian swallowed and then asked, "Could you please give me the name and number of who I should contact?"

"Certainly," responded the receptionist. "Her name is Elise and you can reach her at this same number. She works for Mrs. Claus, too. She's busy right now, but you can try again later, say between four and five, okay? I'll tell Elise to expect your call. Goodbye," she said as she hung up.

"Goodbye," said Ian, "And thanks a lot!"

Ian actually shivered for a few moments after he hung up. "What am I getting myself into?" he thought to himself.

Chapter 5

It took two days before Ian got up enough courage to call Elise. He had asked around his workplace if anybody knew her, but nobody did. Kai thought she was fairly new to Mrs. Claus' office. ("Which would explain why she was still in the support group," Ian thought).

He finally called the receptionist and asked to speak to Elise.

The receptionist said, "Well, of course you can. We've been awaiting your call. Thought maybe you decided not to join the group. Many decide not to. I don't know why this is," she muttered.

"I could give you a few reasons," Ian thought to himself, but didn't say anything to her.

Just then, the sweetest voice Ian had ever heard came on the line.

"Hi, this is Elise. May I help you?" she asked.

Ian gulped. "Uh," he started, "Uh, this is Ian from shipping. I, uh, I'm interested in hearing more about the, uh, support group for cultural studies. The receptionist said you were the one to, uh, contact," he added.

"Yes, I guess that would be me," Elise said. "I missed a meeting once, just when they were looking for somebody to do the secretary stuff and somebody volunteered me," she laughed. "But I really don't mind doing it. I get to meet a lot of new elves," she added.

"And I'm one of them," thought Ian. *"If she's as sweet as she sounds, I can't wait to meet her face to face."*

They chatted for awhile, and Elise asked him a bunch of questions about where he was in his studies and did he have any specific questions, and so on. They decided that, since he was so new to the job, it would be best for him to just start his research. He could use the outline that was available to new shipping elves and start listing his questions.

Ian would also need to start attending the weekly meetings which were on Wednesdays, after work, from six to ten. Mrs. Claus provided dinner for these meetings which the elves really enjoyed. Since it was already Thursday, they hung up saying they would be looking forward to meeting each other at the next Wednesday meeting.

"Yes!" Ian yelled with his fist high in the air. He listened to the background music.

Sometimes when life gets confusing, you know
You have to hang in there and go with the flow
Are you going too fast? Are you going too slow?
You're not really sure. You just don't know.

But one thing you do know and this is for sure
If you give it your best shot, you'll always endure.
So hang in there, Elf, don't throw in the towel
Victory is coming, and soon you will yowl!

"So true," thought Ian as he started his research. First stop –
Europe.

"How is Christmas celebrated in Europe?" Ian thought to
himself.

It was a simple question and one that has been pondered and
talked about for centuries. Because of this, there was a lot of stuff
available for review on the Internet. It was hard to know where to
start. Ian decided to just keep it simple. He'd start with the two
key names: "Christmas" and "Santa Claus."

Ian found that Christmas was really the joining together of two
words – "Christ" and "Mas," (short for Mass). "Christ" is an
English word for the Greek word, "Christos", which means, "The
Anointed One."

"That's great," thought Ian, "But what does "anointed" mean?
So, he did another search and found that "anointed" had three
definitions:

- Anointing used to be a practice of shepherds. Lice and
  other insects would often get into the wool of sheep, and when
  they got near the sheep's head, they could burrow into the
  sheep's ears and kill the sheep. Ancient shepherds poured oil on
  the sheep's head. This made the wool slippery, making it
  impossible for insects to get near the sheep's ears, because they
  would just slide off. From this, "anointing" became a symbol
  of *blessing, protection*, and *empowering*.
- The New Testament Greek word for anoint is "chrio"
  which means "to smear or rub with oil, and by implication to

consecrate   for   office   or   religious   service."
"There's no end to this research stuff," Ian thought. "To consecrate is kind of like *committing yourself* to something. It's like *a ceremony so that others know about it,* too."

- Another meaning for the word "anointed" is "*chosen one.*" The Bible says that Jesus Christ was anointed by God to spread the Good News and to free those who have been held captive by sin.

"Okay," Ian thought. "That's pretty clear. Jesus was/is Christ, or anointed. But what about the "mas" part?"" Further research gave him an answer.

The "mas" part was short for "mass". It meant: "To form or collect into a mass; to form into a collective body; to bring together into masses; to assemble."

"So," Ian thought. "Christmas means that people get together to celebrate the birth of Jesus, the chosen one. Is this true all around the world?"

Later research proved that the answer to this question was not very helpful. It was "yes and no." The "yes" referred to Christians and the "no" to lots of others. Ian thought that this was a question for the support group so he made a note of it in his journal.

Another thought Ian had was, "When you see the name Jesus Christ, you might think that the Christ part was kind of like a last name. But it's not. So if you want to be real picky you might insist that Christ should always come first as in Christ Jesus." Ian decided it could go either way, but if he didn't drop this for now, he was never going to complete any research. So, on with the studies!

Ian concluded that what he found about Jesus Christ, or Christ Jesus, came about because of his European research, but would probably be the same for his research of all the other continents.

The same held true for the word "Christmas."

He added this point to his journal. He hoped that these would be considered "good questions" if he ever had a chance to ask them at a group session.

Okay, so he had a definition of sorts for the word "Christmas", but he still hadn't answered the question "How is Christmas celebrated around the world?" Or, at least in Europe for starters. He decided he'd get to that later. But first, he needed to define "Santa Claus."

Chapter 6

Ian started his research on Santa Claus. This was not an easy chore. The Internet had all kinds of versions of who, or what, Santa Claus really was. But the versions all seemed to characterize him as some sort of mythical character. "He's not a myth," Ian thought. "If I wanted to talk to him right now, all I'd have to do is call him on the phone, or I could even run over to his office, and if he wasn't too busy, I could have a face to face meeting with him. No big deal."

Ian reminded himself that he was supposed to do a simple background review of Santa; not get caught up in what others may think.

Santa varies from country to country, Ian discovered. "That's okay," thought Ian. "Because it's what's passed down from one generation to the next. Very logical, I suppose," Ian continued. Santa Claus is legendary now, but once he lived a rather simple life. His name then was Saint Nicholas. And, before that, it was just plain Nicholas.

Nicholas was born around 280 A.D. in the town of Myra which

is near Patara in modern day Turkey. Actually, Myra was part of Greece at the time of his birth. Nicholas was the child of wealthy parents. At their death they left him a large inheritance. He decided to use his inheritance to help those less fortunate.

He also became a monk and then a bishop. He became the subject of many legends about his gift-giving. One of the best known was about three sisters. They weren't able to marry because they were poor, and in those days, a dowry was required. Ian found that a dowry was a gift that a new bride brought to her new husband or his family. It was a way to get established as a young couple. Ian didn't think much of this idea and decided it wasn't something he'd ever require.

Nicholas heard about the three poor young girls. One night he went to their home, climbed up on the roof and threw three bags of gold down the chimney. Miraculously, a bag fell into each of the sister's stockings, which were hanging by the fireplace to dry after being washed. His kind gift made it possible for all three sisters to marry.

After his death, Nicholas was declared a Saint by the church. He soon became a legend. Legends of his giving spread all over Europe and then throughout the world. With the passing of time, Saint Nicholas became known as Santa Claus in many parts of the world. Ian found that, if he said Saint Nicholas over and over, really fast, it started to sound like Santa Claus!

Ian was sleepy and went to bed. He fell fast asleep and had a dream. In the dream, a beautiful elf brought him a present. He was happy at first, but then she referred to the present as her dowry. This confused Ian and he told her that it wasn't necessary. This apparently hurt her feelings and she ran away, crying. Ian awoke with a start and had a hard time getting back to sleep again, but finally dosed off.

When Ian awoke in the morning he realized he had been researching too hard. He needed a break. He also realized that today was his day off. He felt like doing something active so he gave Samuel a call.

"Hey Samuel, you want to go snowboarding?" he asked. "I heard that the Groomer Elves have the slopes in great shape!"

"Sounds good, Ian," Samuel responded. "In about a half hour, okay?"

"You got it. I'll see you at the lift," Ian said as he hung up.

Ian and Samuel went to their favorite hill. Santa had installed a lift there and it was great not having to trudge up the hillside anymore They had a blast and a lot of their friends were there. Sometimes they raced and sometimes they just cruised. It was a great workout and they both had a wonderful time. "One of the perks of working for Santa," Ian thought.

After they were through snowboarding for the day, they went to the lodge for some hot apple cider. There were lots of elves there enjoying cider and chatting. There was loud music playing and some of the elves were dancing.

Ian knew many of the elves that were there. He also saw some faces he didn't recognize. Some of the men were wearing nice looking ski outfits. Others just wore blue jeans and heavy jackets, with ski goggles on their foreheads and scarves around their necks, trying to look cool.

The girls wore different outfits, too. Some were very cute. Two of them had their heads together and then one of them looked over his way and smiled. Or, at least, he thought it was at him. Maybe someone behind him?

He asked Samuel if he knew her, but Samuel shook his head. Ian figured he didn't have time for girls while he was doing all this heavy research.

That night, before turning in, Ian wrote a summary of where he was in his research and then wrote a *"To Do"* list for the week ahead.

"Okay," he mumbled to himself. "I've done some background on the word Christmas. And I've got a basic version of the origin of the Santa legend," he added. "Now I've got to see how Santa is viewed in other parts of the world. Then I can finish up my review of how Christmas is celebrated in Europe and move on to North America. Man, this is getting tough!"

Chapter 7

Ian got up the next morning and, after breakfast, decided to check his "To Do" list before going to work. It looked okay, but as he was reading the different things he was going to do research on, he started to wonder why he had to know all this stuff. Santa already knew everything, didn't he? And so did Mrs. Claus, didn't she? And all of the other elves that had been around for a long time; they did too, didn't they? He couldn't put a finger on anything. He decided to add this to his list of questions for the support group on Wednesday.

Ian went to work and scrambled as hard as he could and soon had some spare time for research. He couldn't wait to see how Santa Claus was viewed around the world!

He was soon overwhelmed with all the information he found about Santa Claus. He printed out much of what he found so that he could read it later. That night, at dinner, he talked to Samuel about all the stuff he'd found hoping that Samuel could shed some light. "Oh, please tell me!" he thought.

"You know, Ian," Samuel began. "You're so right. There is a

lot of info to study. But one thing you have to realize is that the world hasn't always been "small" the way we consider it today. Mankind has been on earth for thousands of years, but up until a few hundred years ago people lived in their own little villages. They pretty much stayed close to home and if they ever needed to visit somebody in another village, they would either walk or ride an animal, you know, like a horse, or donkey, or whatever. If they came to water, they'd paddle or sail across in a boat."

Samuel continued, "The people developed their own languages and the languages were different. Outside of your own village, you couldn't understand much. But sometimes, people moved. Maybe to find work or to find a place where they could raise animals or grow crops. Some people just wanted to explore. Anyhow, these "movers" were the ones that shared stories, or rumors, or ideas, or whatever."

"Ian," Samuel continued. "Do you remember that time in school when the teacher had the class form a circle? Then she whispered something in the first elf's ear and told him to pass it along. He whispered it to the next elf and so on around the circle. Then she asked the last elf what the message was? It was so funny," Samuel said. "Do you remember?"

"Oh yeah, I remember," Ian chuckled. "The original message was "Santa Claus told Mrs. Claus that he would be late for dinner because he had a meeting with the elves." By the time it got to the last student, the message was "Santa told the elves that Mrs. Claus would be late for the meeting because she was cooking dinner for them." "That was so funny!" Ian snorted as he broke out laughing.

"Yeah, it was," Samuel agreed. "And the point of the exercise was that messages can easily and innocently be changed. It might be that someone in the chain has a hearing problem or maybe talks too fast, or too softly. Or maybe they don't understand some of the vocabulary, but act like they do. You know what I mean?"

"So true," said Ian.

Samuel continued, "Okay, then this is the reason Santa came to be viewed differently around the world. He did all his gift giving secretly and then people would tell others what they thought he looked like, what he ate, how he laughed, and everything else. And, you know what?" Samuel asked. "Santa actually has helpers all around the world, and they take care of the different dates and so on. Isn't that neat?" Samuel asked.

"Yeah, it really is," said Ian. "And I really appreciate you're taking the time to tell me. This will really help my research. Thanks a lot!'

When Ian returned to his research, he felt much better. "So," he thought, "Santa has been around for a long, long time and for most of that time, the world hasn't really been all that small. But now, it is and Santa really needs help keeping track of everything, doesn't he?" he asked himself. As he thought more about how he and the other elves were going to help Santa, he remembered some of the words from Disneyland's "Small World".....

There is just one moon and one golden sun
and a smile means friendship to everyone.
Though the mountains divide
and the oceans are wide
it's a small, small world

Chapter 8

Ian was relieved when he returned to his research. Now he knew why Santa needed his elves, (at least some of them), to be well informed about what was going on in the world.

He waded through all the material he had about how Christmas was celebrated around the world and pulled out his notes about Europe. He had a lot. And now he realized that it just wasn't Santa Claus that was busy on Christmas Eve. Santa had helpers around the world that performed their gift giving in different ways and, in many cases, on different days. For example:

- The Dutch "Sintirklass" arrives by boat on December 6th. Children leave a wooden shoe filled with hay and carrots for the donkey which carries the toys.
- In Italy, "La Befana" is a good witch who dresses all in black. Children leave their shoes by the fireplace on the eve of January 6th. Befana comes down the chimney on her broomstick to leave gifts.

- In Sweden a gnome named "Juletomten" brings gifts in a sleigh driven by goats.
- In England, "Father Christmas" brings gifts on Christmas Eve.
- In France, "Pere Noel" brings gifts to children on Christmas Eve. Children leave their shoes by the fireplace.
- In Denmark, "Julemand" brings gifts on Christmas Eve.
- In many places in Europe, especially Germany, Kris Kringle brings the gifts.
- And in Russia it is Grandfather Frost.

There were so many, many helpers in Europe. "Why does Santa Claus even have to go to Europe," Ian thought to himself. He asked Kai.

"Good question, Ian," Kai began. "I had the same question and here's what I found out. There's a lot of immigration around the world. Since you're studying Europe at the present, let me give you an example.

Let's say that a young French couple moved from Paris to New York. After living there awhile, they became parents. There daughter Yvette grew up and learned about Santa Claus and chose him over Pere Noel. And this was fine.

One year, Yvette went with her parents to visit her grandparents at Christmastime. Of course, this was in Paris. But she had already written a letter to Santa Claus from her address in New York. She told her parents and they told her not to worry, that Santa would find her and, sure enough, he did," Kai ended his story.

"It makes sense to me," said Ian. "And it really did," he thought to himself. The questions that he was saving for Wednesday were starting to be answered.

Ian started thinking about the meeting on Wednesday, which was only two days away. He wasn't looking forward to standing up and doing public speaking. What would he say? How was he supposed to act? Would he be so nervous that they would see him shake? Would they ask lots of questions? Would he be able to answer them?

That night he had nightmare. He saw himself walking up on a stage in front of hundreds of elves who were all looking at him in an unfriendly way. He placed his written speech on the podium in front of him and opened it. The pages were bare! He just stood there, not knowing what to do.

He looked out at the crowd. They were silent but starting to get impatient as they waited for him to begin. Finally he did begin. He decided he'd have to make it up as best as he could.

"Uh, my fellow Elves," he said softly into the microphone. "I've come here today to tell you about Santa Claus. As you know, he is..."

"Turn the mike on!" a voice yelled. "We can't hear a word you're saying!"

Ian nervously fumbled with the microphone, but couldn't get it turned on. "I'm sorry," he said to the crowd. "I can't get this thing to work. I'll speak louder," he said in a louder tone. "Okay," he continued, "As you know, Santa has been around for.."

"We still can't hear you!" the voice boomed. And then everyone started to boo. Ian looked around for help, but nobody came to his aid. He looked out in the crowd. He knew absolutely nobody. He awoke with a start and realized he was having a nightmare. He couldn't get back to sleep. Daybreak finally came and he got up. He was so shook up he could hardly pour milk on his cereal. "This is going to be a long day," he thought.

Chapter 9

Ian trudged slowly to work. He sighed as he sat down at his desk.

Kai looked over at him and asked, "What's up, Ian? Why so glum?"

Ian decided to share his fear of public speaking with Kai. Including the horrible nightmare he'd had last night.

"Pretty typical," Kai said. "I went through the same thing."

"Really?" Ian asked with wide eyes. "Tell me about it."

"Well, I basically had the same fears as you," Kai began. "You know, not being able to remember what I was supposed to talk about. Not able to speak without shaking. Everybody out there waiting for you to make a fool of yourself. You know, all the same things you're worrying about. I know how you feel," he added.

"What did you do?" Ian asked.

"Well, I remember going to my first class, shaking like a leaf," Kai began. "First thing we did was sit down at the dining table in the conference room. There were about fifteen of us. Everybody was talking, except me of course, as dinner was brought in. It was great food from Mrs. Claus' kitchen, but I wasn't at all hungry," Kai continued.

"About the time dessert was being served," Kai said. "Our teacher stood up and addressed us. 'Greetings Class', she began. 'I hope that you've all had a good week. Tonight we're going to continue our sharing presentations. Some of you will tell us a little bit about your own workplace and what it is you do to help Santa in his mission.

We're also going to have some of you present formal speeches. The topic tonight, is the speech to inform. You remember that this speech can be about anything – your choice. But before we start the program, let's go around the room, stand up, say your name and tell us one little known fact about Christmas. Okay, I'll start, she continued. I'm Marie, your teacher. In Australia, during Christmas season, it's actually summer down there in that part of the world so sometimes Santa rides water skis and wears a red bathing suit! The elves laughed loudly.

The next elf continued, 'I'm Robert, from Shipping. In eastern Europe, if kids are naughty, they get coal and onions in their stockings!' 'Oh no!' the elves laughed and groaned.

And so it continued around the room. Finally, it got to me," Kai said. "I didn't have anything funny to say so I just said, 'I'm Kai, from Shipping. This is my first night and I still have a lot to learn, but I'm looking forward to meeting you all.'

And with that," Kai said, "they all stood up and applauded and yelled welcome and stuff like that. Let me tell you, it made me feel a whole lot better!"

Kai went on to tell how the typical class sessions were set up. How everybody got a chance to say something. Sometimes, they would be in the main group for the speeches or other presentations. Sometimes, they would work in small groups. And sometimes, in pairs. The variety was good. There were lots of activities and games. "It was actually a lot of fun, at times," Kai said.

"How many speeches did you have to make during your ten weeks of class?" Ian asked.

"We each had to prepare three formal speeches and present them to the main group," Kai began. "The first was a speech to inform, that had to last from 15 to 20 minutes. Mine was titled 'Ice Hockey at the North Pole' and compared it to ice hockey in other places around the world. The second was a speech to create emotions, for five to ten minutes, and I talked about the three sisters before they were helped by Saint Nicholas.

And the final speech," Kai concluded, "was a speech to make elves laugh. This was also for five to ten minutes. My subject was about a penguin trying to fly. He couldn't make his wings work the way other birds did, so he finally gave up trying to fly and decided he'd learn to walk fast instead."

"That really sounds funny!" Ian laughed. "How did it turn out?"

"Well, the speech might not have been as funny as my bodily actions, but nobody seemed to care," Kai laughed. "I'd say that it went okay and that I felt good about it."

"Besides the three speeches," Kai continued. "We had to do short presentations in support of answers to questions that would come up. This was voluntary, but one of you had to answer before the teacher moved on to the next subject. Several times we had to stay long after ten o'clock!"

"Ouch, that's no good!" said Ian. "Hey, Kai," he continued. "One more question, okay?" "You bet!" said Kai.

"Why do we have to do all this public speaking, anyhow?" Ian asked in a frustrated tone.

"Haw, I was wondering when you'd get to that one," laughed

Kai. "Let me tell you few reasons now and they'll tell you the rest in class. There's a bunch of reasons."

"First of all," Kai began. "By taking this training, you'll learn how to be a more skilled and sensitive communicator. It will encourage you to look inside yourself and explore what matters to you and then to share your thoughts in a way that listeners will understand. You'll learn to consider your listeners – what do they want, need, like, care about? You'll learn to speak out in important situations and to give or get help in class. Make sense?"

"Yeah," Ian responded. "The way you put it, it makes a lot of sense."

Kai's description of his early speech problems made Ian feel a lot better and he was able to concentrate on his research again. He borrowed a globe from the warehouse and started studying it intensely. He would slowly spin it and play like he was Santa going around the world. It seemed easy enough, but then the globe was very small and didn't have all the mountains and canyons and stuff like that. "Those are the things that could really make it confusing," he thought.

Chapter 10

Since Ian was pretty much done with his research of Europe, he decided that Santa would probably head over the North Pole. He might stop at Iceland on his way over. Then go to Alaska and then zigzag across Canada, Greenland, the United States, Mexico, and Central America.

Ian then scratched his head and thought to himself, "When Santa is done with Central America, would he continue on down to South America or would he head over to Asia by way of Hawaii?" He decided to call Samuel.

"Hey, Samuel," Ian said. "I've got another question. Got a minute?"

"Yeah, no problem, Ian," Samuel responded. "What can I do for you?"

"I'm trying to figure out which way Santa would go on Christmas Eve. Since I'm currently studying Christmas celebrations in Europe, I was trying to decide Santa's next stop. Got any ideas, Samuel?" Ian asked.

"Well, first of all, since we're all at the North Pole," Samuel began. "That is, you, me, Santa, you know, all of us, we're at the top of the world. This is where all the time zones come together," he added. "So the first thing Santa does is choose a time zone."

"I don't want to sound like a complete dummy," Ian said. "But could you please tell me what a time zone is?"

"Okay, but let me put it in simple Christmas Eve terms," Samuel chuckled. "Let's forget time zones. They're too confusing. Here's the situation. Santa needs to reach everybody on Christmas Eve. So he starts with the countries that experience Christmas Eve first and then he works his way in a westerly direction. And he zigzags up and down. Does this make sense?"

"Well, kind of," said Ian. "Could you give me an example?"

"Okay," Samuel said. "First of all, would you agree that, from Santa's point of view, Christmas Eve begins around the time that most of the kids are in bed, asleep? Let's say around 9:00 P.M.?"

"Yeah," said Ian. "That sounds reasonable.

"Okay, then," Samuel continued. "Santa would start with the first area in the world to reach 9:00 P.M. on Christmas Eve. This would be, in the northern hemisphere, eastern Russia and in the southern hemisphere, New Zealand or the Fiji Islands."

"Okay," Ian said. "Then where would he go?"

"Well, this is really Santa's decision, but to kind of clear it up for you, let's say Santa came down from the North Pole to eastern Russia and then continued down to the Fiji Islands. After Fiji, he might continue down to New Zealand and then over to Australia, and up to Indonesia, the Philippines, Japan, China, more of eastern Russia, and so on. This really makes more sense if you have a globe, or even a flat map is helpful" Samuel said. "What do you think? Does this make sense?"

Ian stuck his fist up in the air and yelled, "Yes!"

Later he put together a plan that would have two main items: (1)

Research on Christmas and Santa Claus celebrations around the world and (2) A trip plan that would get Santa from point to point in a logical way. "Maybe Santa already has a plan," Ian thought. "But it won't hurt to have a backup plan." And so he got to work. It was early evening, he'd already had dinner and now he could get into some serious research on the net. Just then, his phone rang.

He answered it and heard that beautiful voice of Elise again. "Ian," she began. "Hi, this is Elise. How are you?"

"Fine," Ian answered. He fished for words. "Uh, how about you?"

"Oh, I'm fine, too," Elise continued. "I'm calling everybody to remind them of the Support Group meeting tomorrow night."

"Oh, that's right," Ian answered.

"Tomorrow night a couple of guys will be doing speeches to infirm," Elise said. "Have you heard anything about this?"

"Yeah, fortunately, a guy that works right across from me was in the group a couple of years ago and he gave me a pretty good rundown on what goes on," Ian answered.

"Oh, that's wonderful," Elise responded. "And so typical of graduates from the group. They're always there to help out. Oh, I'm so thrilled! Could I ask who it was?"

"Certainly," Ian answered. "His name is Kai and I'll tell you, I'm lucky to have him working right across from me. He's really a good guy and is always there to help out."

"Great!" Elise said. "And it's making my job tonight very easy, too!" she laughed. "Do you have any questions, Ian?"

"Gosh," Ian thought. *"She says my name in such a sweet way. I can't wait to meet her."* "Probably, I do," Ian answered. "But I can't think of them right now. Uh, Elise," he asked. "Will you, uh, be there tomorrow?"

"Why, of course," she said. "I'm the one that got volunteered to do this secretarial stuff. Make sure that you never miss a meeting," she laughed. "Well then, Ian, I'll see you tomorrow. It starts at six. Don't be late," she giggled.

"Okay, Elise," Ian responded. "See you tomorrow." And they hung up.

Ian was smiling as he returned to his studies. He decided his original plan of going west to North America from Europe was no longer good. The trip plan was now heading in the opposite direction. "Oh well," he thought. "I didn't really get going on the other one so it's no big deal."

"Maybe I should see if I can find a little known fact about Christmas or Santa to share with the group tomorrow night," he thought. "I don't want to look like a complete dummy."

Chapter 11

Ian awoke early after a restless night's sleep. He was worried about the support group meeting tonight. "My first, and maybe my last, if I don't perform to their expectations," he thought as he assembled all the notes that he thought he'd need for the meeting. "The thing is, I don't really know what I'll need, so I guess I'll just bring it all. I can keep it in my back pack."

The day was a blur for him at work. He couldn't keep his mind on anything other than worrying. Fortunately, the workload was light and he had some time to do some research on Christmas culture in eastern Russia, New Zealand, Fiji Islands, and Australia.

In eastern Russia, many people celebrate Christmas with twelve course dinners and a visit by Grandfather Frost who has a granddaughter to help him!

"Hooray for the helpers!" Ian yelled as he turned another page.

In New Zealand, Ian discovered, the Christmas traditions originally came with early settlers from England in the 18th century. They used to be visited by Father Christmas, but now many of the kids write to Santa Claus instead. "We're flexible," Ian thought. "But I better alert Santa so he can expect an increase in the number of deliveries he'll have to make in New Zealand from now on." Ian found Australia to be a lot like New Zealand. They both had the migration of people from England, and they both had existing Polynesian people there before the arrival of the immigrants. They liked to celebrate too, and mixed their culture with the British culture. It was confusing to an outsider, but fun!

When Ian looked at the Fiji Islands, he was surprised to find that it was a country with many cultures and races. This meant there were many different religions and many different ways to celebrate Christmas. Santa would be busy, but so would all of the helpers. "Probably not any surprises for Santa here," Ian concluded as he looked at his watch. "I'd better wrap this research up for the day and start getting ready for class," he thought as he looked at his watch again. "I wish I wasn't so nervous. It's just a class with a few other elves. I wonder how many there'll be?"

Ian showered and got dressed in his best outfit. He tucked his black pants into his boots and then slipped on a tan woolen long-sleeve shirt. He did not tuck the shirt in because it had belt loops to hold a black leather belt with a large, shiny buckle. His boots were typical elf boots with pointed, curled up toes and high tops which folded over. They were made of soft brown leather with some red trim around the top. His hat was made of the same soft brown leather and it had a bright red head band and a matching red tassel. He looked in his hallway mirror. He was ready!

Ian walked over to the recreation hall where the elves could hang out in their spare time. It had a basketball court, a bowling alley, a pool room with several pool tables, a computer room, library, snack shop, and a large dining hall that was used for special functions, meetings, and training. The front part, where the play areas were located, was very noisy with the sounds of basketball games or tennis matches, or pool games with the players and spectators yelling their support or disagreement! As Ian proceeded deeper into the building, the noise level got to be less and less as he passed the computer room and library. Finally, he reached the back and stood in front of the entrance to the training room. It was about a quarter to six but there were several elves already in there, standing around and talking. Ian looked up over the entrance and saw a wooden plaque with words inscribed in gold.

"Your Hands and Your Hearts Make it Possible"

One of Ian's friends, a young elf named James, had composed a song. It was selected by Santa to be played at the Opening Ceremony for the new recreation building.

"Lend me your hands
If willing, today
Lend me your hearts
To help pave the way"

"Let's sit a moment
To ponder our load
The Naughty and Nice List
Is here, let's unfold"

"The "Nice" list is long
And the "Naughty" is short
But sometimes a "Nice" one
Has a "Naughty" cohort"

"Let's hope we can help
The "Naughties" change course
And bring joy to their parents
(We'll hear them rejoice!)"

"So on with the list
We've got lots to achieve
Let's get it all finished
Before Christmas Eve"

Chorus
"We know we've been faithful
We know we've been true
We know you are calling
There's much work to do."

Ian remembered when Santa had dedicated this building to the elves a few years ago. He did it in recognition of their hard work and their caring hearts. All the elves were very proud of this. Over time, a greeting amongst them became very popular and you often heard it as a kind of symbol of support or recognition. Whenever you heard "H & H, Dude!" or "H & H, Girl!" you always, (that is, if you were an elf), paused in what you were doing, smiled, and raised your right fist. Ian smiled to himself. He was proud to be an elf. With that thought, he walked into the dining hall to start his training.

Chapter 12

As Ian entered the conference room, there was a large table in the middle of the room and several groups of elves standing around talking. The table was set for dinner, but the teacher was working on something on the podium at the head of the table. She was adjusting some wires and kept tapping on the face of the microphone, but nothing came out. This brought back a memory of a nightmare. "Just what I need," Ian thought. He gazed around the room, trying to decide how many were there. Looked like around twenty.

Ian walked over to another elf that was standing alone. He held out his hand to shake and said, "Hi, my name is Ian."

"Pleased to meet you," the other guy said. "My name is Robert."

They both looked quickly at each other's name tag as if to confirm that the names were right.

"This is my first night," Ian said. "How about you?"

"This is my fifth night," Robert said with a weary look on his face. "I'm half way done. I did my speech to amuse last week."

"How'd it go?" Ian asked.

"I don't know. I guess it was okay," Robert said with a straight face. "We have to wait until the tenth, you know, the last session before we get any feedback from the teacher. She doesn't want us to worry about it. That's fine with me," he said.

"This is my first night," Ian said smiling nervously. "There looks to be about twenty in the class."

Ian gazed around the class while he was talking and made a quick count. The groups weren't mixed at all. There were either all guys or all gals except for one. In this group, there was one girl surrounded by a bunch of guys. She had a clipboard and was calling their names. Ian realized that she was taking the attendance and talking about something else which Ian couldn't hear because her back was toward him. Finally, she broke away from the group, looked down at her clipboard, and did some counting to herself. Then, she looked up, gazed around the room, nodded their way, and started walking toward them.

As she got close to them, Ian realized that he had seen her somewhere before. She was really cute and when she got close enough Ian could read her name tag. It was Elise! She was the one at the ski lodge!

"Hi, Robert!" she began. "And you must be Ian!" she exclaimed with a big smile. She reached out and shook their hands. "Well, this is the night, isn't it? She asked jokingly. "There's no turning back now!"

Ian kind of winced at her words, but tried not to show it too much.

"Yeah, I know," he said with a sheepish grin. "This is it!"

"I've been taking attendance and also making sure that the scheduled speakers are ready to go," Elise said. "Let's see, you're all done with your three speeches, aren't you, Robert?" she asked.

"Oh, yeah!" Robert exclaimed with a big smile. "I am soooo done!"

"And, Ian," Elise began. "I know you haven't had a chance to talk to the teacher yet, but she'll corner you before the night's over and let you know that you're scheduled for a 'Speech to Inform' next week. Do you have a subject yet?" she asked with a smile.

"I'm almost there," Ian answered with a questioning look on his face that turned into a half smile. "I'll be ready."

Just then, they heard a loud microphone squeak, a couple of sputters and then, "Okay, class, dinner is served!"

There was a mad scramble to the table.

Ian started to follow Elise, but she mentioned in a hushed tone, "Ian, I have to sit up front, next to Marie, the teacher, because I have to take notes for minutes, you know. But, when you do your speeches, you'll get to sit there, too and we'll be able to talk. But tonight, just find a seat that's available."

Ian followed Robert to the table and they sat down.

"Welcome, everybody," Marie spoke into the microphone. "We've got a full schedule ahead, so we'd better get going. Mrs. Claus has prepared one of her favorites for us tonight. Let's eat!"

Chapter 13

Ian couldn't believe how delicious everything was. The meal was extra-special. Mrs. Claus, of course, supervised everything that came out of her kitchen, but for special events, she went all out. That meant she personally took part in the preparation. The recipes she used were all in her head and they were from all over the world. The dinners for the Cultural Studies Support Group functions were clearly among her favorites.

Everybody was quiet while eating and this suited Ian fine. He had never been good at making conversation. At least with strangers. He sat next to Robert, who was quiet himself, so they just ate and waited for things to begin. The food servers were starting to pick up the dinner plates and making room for dessert.

Ian looked around the table while the servers were busy. He had seen several of the student elves around, but really didn't know any of them. He noticed Elise talking to the teacher, showing her the attendance, and other stuff she had on her clipboard. Elise really seemed to be well organized, *"besides being cute,"* Ian thought to himself.

As Ian was gazing down their way, Teacher Marie nodded to Elise and then rose.

"Good evening, students," she said. "Welcome to another session of the CSS. Tonight, as always, we have a full schedule so we'd better get going. While we're enjoying our dessert, let's go around the room and introduce ourselves and present to the class a little known fact about Christmas or Santa Claus. Who wants to start?"

Several hands went up and Teacher Marie pointed to a blond elf, named Haley.

"Okay, let's start with you. Please rise and introduce yourself and tell us something new," she said while chuckling.

Haley stood up, and while she was looking around the table, she began, "Hi, everyone. My name is Haley and I work in Accounting."

A couple of elves laughingly yelled, "Go, Accounting!"

Haley smiled and turned a little red but continued, "Santa brings us all together! Kids all over the world know who Santa is. And although he may be a little commercial, who can help, but love the jolly old elf? It's the idea of giving that reminds us; we are all on this planet together, for the long run. So let's be kind to one another."

Normally, the elves would be expecting a humorous fact about Santa so they were quiet for a moment. Haley looked around with a nervous look on her face, but then the clapping started and grew louder and lasted longer than usual. It was accompanied by yells, too! The other students appreciated what she had just said. She sat down with a happy smile on her face.

The introductions continued around the table. There were lots of laughs and hoots. The elves really enjoyed this part of the training session. Finally it was Ian's turn.

"Hello, everyone," Ian began. "My name is Ian. I work in Shipping and as you all know, this is my first night. I'm really enjoying your little bits of info about Santa and Christmas. Here's another one for you. Before settling on the name of Tiny Tim for his character in *A Christmas Carol,* three other names were considered by Charles Dickens. They were Little Larry, Puny Pete, and Small Sam."

Ian smiled a nervous smile and sat down. That was it! It was over! He had made his first presentation and he was still alive!

The elves liked the way he handled the presentation and because he was new, they stood and applauded him and yelled out, "Way to go!" "Welcome!" "Puny Pete? You've gotta be kidding!" "Go Shipping!" and other friendly gestures. Ian also heard a "You'll be sorry!" He didn't mind, but laughed instead, and raised his fist in the air. He felt so good!

The rest of the night was kind of a blur. Things happened so quickly, but in an orderly manner. He listened to several speeches and a couple of presentations in small groups. Near the end, the teacher had them pair up and discuss their plans for the next meeting. At this point, she invited Ian over to a corner table and he got his first orientation.

"Well, Ian," Teacher Marie began. "How is everything going for you so far? Is this what you expected?"

"It's actually more than I expected," Ian began.

"Tell me about it," Teacher Marie prodded.

"First of all, everything is so well organized. Having twenty elves in one room at the same time without mass chaos is certainly a tribute to the program," Ian chuckled. "Also, everyone gets a chance to participate right from the start. You feel like you belong."

"I'm glad you feel that way," Teacher Marie said. "That's what we try to do. To have an orderly program and encourage everyone to add to it and feel like it's theirs. Sounds like it's working for you and I'm happy to hear that."

"Okay, Ian," Teacher Marie said in a soft voice. "Let me tell you a bit about the Cultural Studies Support Group. By the way, we usually refer to it as just CSS." She continued, "CSS was formed several years ago when it became apparent that the world was indeed getting smaller and smaller, and at a very rapid pace. People aren't staying in the places where they were born for very long. There continues to be lots of migration. And, as smart as Santa is, he's having a challenge to keep up with everything. Fortunately, he has lots of helpers around the world and then, of course, there's us elves. So far, so good?" Teacher Marie asked.

"Yes, Ms. Marie," Ian answered.

"Great," Teacher Marie continued. "Now, let me tell you where you fit in. We elves are key to this equation. We happily help Santa succeed by keeping him informed of changes in the world cultures that might impact him. We all contribute, to the best of our abilities, and Santa is so happy about this."

"But some of us have different skills to offer," Teacher Marie waved her arm around the room as she spoke. "I like to teach while others like to work in shipping like you. Some like to cook and they work in Mrs. Claus' kitchen. Still others like to keep records, or pack toys, or clean the factories. I could go on and on, but you get what I mean, don't you?" she asked.

Ian nodded yes. Teacher was on a roll and he didn't want to interrupt.

"So, what I guess I'm trying to say is this – that the elves need coordination too. They need help just like Santa needs their help. They need leaders," and as she said this, she looked straight into Ian's eyes.

"You guys and gals in training have been selected because of your leadership potential," she said. "Actually, in your case, it's a combination of things: Inter-personal skills, dedication to the job, and research capabilities."

Ian's heart did a flip-flop, but he continued listening intently.

"You and the others in class have differing skills and interests, but there's one thing you all have in common; you are the cream of the crop, the best of the best," Teacher Marie continued. "We'd like to help you become even better!"

"With all of my fumbling around with different jobs," Ian said. "I never expected anything like this." He looked at Teacher Marie with a questioning look on his face.

"Some elves accept their fate without question. Others decide to do something about what the hand of fate has dealt them. These are the elves that get noticed by the candidate selection team," Teacher Marie continued with a smile. "Now, this doesn't mean that you have to be a manager. You can get out at any time and there'll be no hard feelings. We don't need your decision right now. Think it over. I'm sure you'll come to the decision that fits you. And I'm sure that it'll be soon," she said knowingly.

Ian's head was spinning as he walked home after class. "A manager? A Leader? Me?"

What do I have to do with my life if I want to learn to lead?
I often wonder what it'll take if I'm really going to succeed.

Management rules are based upon processes, order, control
You can't just do a part of them; you've got to do the whole.

Leadership, on the other hand, is expressing human spirit
And to become a successful leader, you have to want to do it.

How then, I ask myself, will I know when I have become one?
The answer is really simple Elf; you'll soon be having more fun.

Leadership is a process whereby leaders and followers unite
To accomplish lots of mutual goals that need to be just right

We are all leaders and followers at different points in time
Can't have one without the other, you know, it just won't rhyme.

Elves express their leadership when they act as part of a whole
And to really be successful, then you've got to know your role.

To discover a role in this elf's world you have to be part of the
group
You have to work together as a soldier does in a troop.

So, in this journey of discovery your aim has got to be this:
To develop the potential in others and to promise you won't be
remiss.

Chapter 14

Ian woke up early and couldn't get back to sleep so he decided to just get up and get ready for work. His head started to spin again as he thought about his meeting with Teacher Marie. He needed to talk to somebody. He would call Samuel later during his break.

"Hey Samuel, how's it going?" Ian asked.

"Everything's fine," Samuel responded. "How'd your class go last night?"

"It was unbelievable!" Ian said. He told Samuel everything that had happened including his orientation session with Teacher Marie.

"Could you picture me as a manager?" Ian asked laughing.

"Well, to be quite honest, I could," Samuel answered. "You're bright, honest, fair, and have good instincts. And, you've got a sense of humor. The thing you have to answer to yourself is whether you truly want to be a manager. If so, then everything else will come together for you and you'll be successful. Simple as that," he added.

They talked some more and then they both had to get back to work. Ian decided to ask Kai the same question. He did and got practically the same answer.

"Kai, what did you decide to do?" Ian asked. "After all, you went to the CSS training too."

"Yeah, that's true," Kai said. "But you know, one of the things you have to answer is whether you're willing to accompany Santa Claus on a trip. I had to say no because I'm afraid of heights. I don't know why, but I am," he added sadly. "I will still be able to go into management, but will just have to wait for an opening. Meanwhile, I'm happy where I am," he added with a smile.

Ian wondered whether he was afraid of heights. When they went on the ski lift, he got excited, but didn't think it was from fear. Who else could he ask?

Samuel didn't want to be in the management ranks although he would certainly be successful. Robert didn't seem real excited about the program. He didn't want to ask Marie at this point. Who else could he ask that he felt could give him some good advice? Then it came to him. Elise!

If she couldn't give him direct advice, she would certainly know whom he could ask. He decided to give her a call. She had given him her direct line at the class in case he had any questions about anything.

"Hi, Ian!" Elise said when she picked up the line and saw that it was him. "Well, are you recovered from last night?" She laughed.

"I think so," he answered. "I had my orientation with Ms. Marie and she told me all about the reason we were selected. Were you surprised when you first learned?" he asked.

"Well, actually, no," she said. "You know, when you work for Mrs. Claus there aren't any secrets. Everybody knows everything that's going on, at least in her kitchen. She loves to talk while she works and well, I guess we do too," she giggled. "Anyhow, I found out about my selection long before my class started, so I had time to think about it and ask questions beforehand. I understand what you're going through right now, so fire away!"

"I guess the biggest question I have is whether or not I want to be a manager. I had never really thought about it until last night. What about you? Have you made your decision?" Ian asked.

"I have," Elise answered. "I'm going for it!"

"You sound very sure of yourself," Ian said. "Did you ever have any doubts?"

"Yeah, I think I did at first, but then I started thinking about what managers really can do," Elise began. "How they can help others succeed. This is what really got me excited. I don't care about the power and position. This comes with the job, I know, but it's not something that should be abused. You know, power for power's sake? Anyhow," Elise added with a smile in her voice. "I'm happy I made the decision to become a manager and I'm looking forward to getting going. Does this help?"

"Yes, it does," Ian answered. He noticed that he didn't stutter anymore when he talked to her. She was easy to get along with. "I'm glad I called," he added.

"I am too," she answered softly. "Oh, by the way, did you select a topic for your first speech?"

"Yeah, I have," Ian answered. "I'm going to talk about navigation. You know, how early explorers got around and what kind of tools and technology are used today. I'll include Santa's techniques, too."

"Sounds really interesting," Elise said. "I'm looking forward to your presentation next week. Navigation is like Greek to me. I don't have a clue how it works. Nobody knows how Santa does it, either. He just says, "Good eyes, a calculating mind, and Rudolph" and of course, he always adds, "Ho, Ho, Ho!" Elise continued, "I heard that one of the manager elves suggested that Santa outfit his sleigh with a navigation system, but Santa said no, that it wasn't needed and that was that."

"Oh, really?" Ian exclaimed. "When was that?"

"I'm not sure. Quite a few years ago, I think." Elise offered.

"What I wonder is, what would Santa do if Rudolph couldn't help for whatever reason?" Ian asked solemnly.

There was a long silence at the other end and then Elise answered slowly and in a serious tone, "Well, I guess he'd, uh, (pause), gosh, I'm afraid I can't answer that question. What would you do, Ian?"

"I'm not sure," Ian responded. "But maybe it's time to look at a navigation system again. I'll see what my research produces and we'll go from there."

Ian and Elise chatted a few more minutes and then said goodbye and hung up.

Chapter 15

Ian did a lot of research for the next few days. He had two missions now. One was to prepare a speech for Wednesday's CSS meeting. The second was to see if there was some kind of navigation system that Santa could rely on when he made his Christmas Eve deliveries.

Navigation in the early days of mankind was interesting, Ian discovered. It started around 3500 BC when people started trading. The first traders stayed close to shore. They knew all the ins and outs of the shorelines and only traded during the day. If they couldn't make it home before dark, they would find a sheltered cove and stay there for the night. "Simple enough," Ian muttered. "But it was a start."

With the passage of time, navigators used the sun and stars to help them determine where they were. "I'm pretty sure that Santa relies on the stars," Ian thought. "Especially the North Star."

Another navigation system that came into being over time was called "dead reckoning." Using this system, a navigator could determine the distance traveled from one point to another by estimating the speed of his boat and calculating the passage of time by using a sand glass. "Let's see," Ian thought. "A sand glass is a device that some folks still use in the kitchen when they boil an egg or something. You turn it upside down and it takes a certain number of minutes for all the sand to drop into the bottom container."

"But how did they know how fast their boat was going?" Ian wondered as he continued his search. And then he found it! The navigator would estimate the speed of the boat by watching pieces of seaweed pass by the hull!

"Okay," Ian thought. "Now I see!" He was getting excited! "If the seaweed speed tells you that your boat is going three miles per hour and it takes you ten hours to get to your destination, then you multiply the speed by the time, or three times ten, and you've gone thirty miles! You can record this in your journal and you'll have that information forever! Santa probably uses this dead reckoning system, too, but it's probably all in his head."

As Ian continued his study of navigation, he started to wonder how he was going to cram all this information into a fifteen to twenty minute speech. Also, if you give the listeners too many details, you'll lose their attention. What he decided to do was to include a discussion of the early navigation systems, like sun, stars, and dead reckoning. Then he would skip pretty fast through all the devices that were invented over the years and put the most emphasis on modern technology. He thought this over for several minutes and then nodded yes to himself.

One item he came across as very simple and interesting was used by the Vikings. They would often bring along a crate of birds, called ravens. When they thought they might be getting close to land, they would release one of the ravens. If it kept circling around their boat, they knew they weren't close to land. But if the bird took off, it was heading for land!

Another item of information from the Vikings is that their preferred sailing season was the summertime. Warm temperatures, sun high in the sky, good weather. Ian thought about Santa's trips in the dead of winter…

The Vikings may have used a "sunstone" to help them navigate, but historians are still arguing about whether this was true or not, so Ian decided to drop it.

In about the 13th Century, the compass was invented, which really helped navigating when the weather blocked out the sun or stars. Also about this time, came the invention of the "lead" line. This was a tool that measured the depth of the water. Navigators kept records and could estimate where they were by the depth.

In the Mediterranean, the sailors were often guided by bonfires built for them on distant shores by their comrades.

Maps started to be made around the 13th century, and were very useful from then on.

Ian found all kinds of interesting devices invented over the years, which he decided he wouldn't have time in his speech to describe. He needed to fast forward to the world today! He did so and reached GPS.

GPS stands for Global Positioning System and was invented in the early 1970's. As Ian read a little more, his eyes got big and he started to smile. The system consists of twenty four satellites. They send out signals from space and you can use a receiver to determine where you are anywhere on earth.

"Yes!" Ian yelled!

Since its invention, GPS has been improved with each passing year, and now the receivers are so simple and small that they can be included in a cell phone! Ian decided to buy one, so he went online and ordered a cell phone equipped with GPS. It wouldn't be there in time for his speech, but it wouldn't be a problem. He'd have it soon enough to show Santa and see if he might convince him to equip his sleigh with one of them for Christmas Eve.

Long, long ago, some Vikings ventured out
To see the world as others did; what was it all about?
They sailed all day, they sailed all night, so far away from home
They used the sun and many stars and reckoning to roam.

They saw Iceland and Greenland and many other lands
They used their sails when windy, but often used their hands
They paddled with a vision and knew that they would reach
A new land with green trees and a bright golden beach.

When their roaming days were over and they settled down again
They found their homes in many lands with challenges and then
They told their stories gladly for they were very proud
They'd found a silver lining to put upon their cloud.

Chapter 16

Before he knew it, Wednesday had arrived, and that night, Ian had to present his first speech. Unfortunately, his mind was racing with all kinds of negative thoughts. He remembered his nightmare where the pages were blank and the mike wouldn't work. He tried to relax, but it was impossible. His speech seemed to be okay on paper. Now, if he could just deliver it…

When Ian arrived at class, the same groups were chatting and laughing as he remembered from last week. He didn't know which one to join and kind of hesitated. He remembered recently having read some consultant's writings about how to function in a situation that was very similar to this.

First of all, the consultant advised, remember that everyone at this event probably has the same interests, and fears, as you. There's lots of common ground. Secondly, you should introduce yourself rather than wait for them to introduce themselves. After all, they're probably all just as nervous as you are. That's why they get into their small groups. Third point, do something that the host needs to have done. In other words, transfer yourself from guest to host.

Just then, Ian spotted Elise going around the room from group to group with her clipboard. Maybe he could help her out and start to act like a host?

"Hi, Elise," Ian said to her between groups. "You're working too hard. Can I give you a hand?"

A big smile broke out on Elise's face. "That would be wonderful!" She exclaimed. "I don't know what happened, but I am so far behind and class is about ready to begin! Okay, if you could take the roll, then I can focus on getting the speeches scheduled. By the way, are you ready? You're third tonight, you know."

"Yeah, I'm ready, I think," Ian grinned nervously.

"Good," Elise said. "You know what? I'm going to make an announcement that you'll be taking roll. It'll go faster if they know what's going on."

Elise ran to the front podium, turned on the mike and announced, "Fellow students, may I have your attention for a moment? Ian has volunteered to help me take roll tonight so we can get back on schedule. So make sure you say "here!" when he comes around and calls your name. Oh, and you can give him a smile, too! Thanks for helping, Ian!"

With that, she turned off the mike and went about her business. Ian was on his own, but now he was a host with a plan!

As Ian went around the room taking roll, the student groups welcomed him with their smiles and their jokes about him being roped into service by Elise. "Little do they know," he thought with a smile on his face.

Since Ian was to be one of the speakers, he had to sit up front, near the podium. Elise saved a seat for him next to her. They chatted a little during dinner, but dinner went by too fast. Then Teacher Marie got things going. There were the self-introductions,

78

a few announcements, and then the speakers began.

There were two speakers in front of Ian and he had a hard time paying attention to them because he was thinking about his own presentation. "This is the one," he thought. "This is it! There's no turning back now!" And then he heard himself being introduced. He rose and walked to the podium with notes in hand.

He placed his notes on the podium and glanced at the first page. It wasn't bare! He could read it! He smiled broadly with relief and then spoke into the microphone. "Good evening everyone," he said. He heard his voice resonate! The mike worked! He smiled broadly again and now his smiles were starting to make others smile as well, so when Ian gazed around, he felt like he was surrounded by true friends!

Feeling a lot more comfortable and relaxed, Ian began his speech. "Okay, everybody," Ian began. "Let's go back in time, way back to about 3500 BC. Close your eyes for a moment and try to picture how simple everyday life was. You lived in a small coastal village where all of your family lived and where all of your ancestors before you had lived. You fished and you raised crops and animals for food and clothing. Life was good.

Then one year you had a great harvest. The crops were super and the animal herds and even the fishing was great. You had more food and hides for clothing than you could use. What should you do with the extra?

Someone suggested that maybe they could load a boat and go to the next village up the coast and maybe they would trade something for the extra goods. So they did this. My fellow elves," Ian proclaimed. "This was the day that changed the world! This was the beginning of the age of trading; something that would go on forever!"

Ian then went on to describe how the traders used the different navigation techniques to get them from one place to another. He covered a lot of the info he had researched, but made sure he stuck to the twenty-minute limit. He ended up emphasizing GPS and explained it in simple terms. As he concluded, he asked if there were any questions.

Paul, an elf from one of the toy factories, raised his hand and Ian pointed at him, saying, "Yes, Paul?"

"I was just wondering," Paul began. "If you think the Christmas Eve sleigh ought to be equipped with GPS?"

"Good question, Paul," Ian answered slowly. "I've heard that Santa doesn't like the idea. He said it's not really necessary. I'm planning on presenting the idea to him once again and we'll see."

Ian sat down after his presentation and it felt as if the weight of the world had been removed from his shoulders. Elise looked over at him, smiled, and whispered, "Good job!"

Chapter 17

Ian continued his research during his spare time or his off hours. He enjoyed getting on the Internet and "googling" away. He stayed on course, too. After leaving Australia, he traveled north through Indonesia and up into the heart of Asia: China, India, Russia, and a whole bunch of other, smaller, but still interesting, countries. He knew that the other student elves were doing the same kind of searches because they shared lots of information at their weekly meetings. "This CSS group was a great idea!" Ian mentioned to Teacher Marie at their weekly one on one meeting.

"Glad you like it, Ian" she said. "You know, we give Santa a briefing each week on the things that are discussed. He really appreciates the new data that is provided. Helps him carry out his mission."

"Ms.Marie ," Ian began. "Do you think I can get in to see Santa and talk to him about GPS?"

"I'm afraid not, Ian," she answered. "We told him about your idea but he is convinced that his own basic navigation skills are enough and then, like he says, he's always got Rudolph. Maybe someday he'll listen, but I'm afraid the answer now is no. Sorry."

Ian was disappointed, but he didn't let it bother him for long. He was having too good a time with his research, his class, and getting to know the student elves better. They were a great group. So smart! So dedicated! They worked hard and they played hard!

About midway through the ten week session, someone in class suggested that they all meet for a day of skiing, or snow-boarding, followed by some dinner, singing and dancing at the lodge. There was a unanimous vote in favor!

It was a beautiful day at the ski runs. Everybody came prepared to give it their best. They were all dressed up in their ski outfits and they soon started racing down the slopes. Some were on skis; some on snow-boards. It didn't matter. They played games, whooped and hollered and had a great time!

When they rode up the ski lifts, they got to visit with all the different elves in the class – young men and young ladies. Everybody got to know everybody else and in such an enjoyable way. Even Teacher Marie was out there, and she was having a ball!

Ian decided to ski this time, rather than snow board. He had been doing both for years and liked to change once in awhile. Elise was a skier today too and so they rode up the lift together quite a bit. They talked about everything, mostly about the class, but also about their jobs, their lives, their friends, other students, and their futures.

Elise would graduate before Ian and she thought that she probably would return to Mrs. Claus' operations, but she really wasn't sure. Once you get into management at the North Pole, you can go just about anywhere, sometimes even to other parts of the world, when needed, to work with Santa's Helpers.

Besides being trained in the culinary arts as a chef, Elise had also been trained as an Emergency Medical Technician. Some people call them paramedics, others call them medics. But, basically she was trained to respond to elves requiring first aid because of work related injuries or to help them in the early stages of a common cold. Even Santa had been known to catch the sniffles once in awhile! And, as everyone knows, if you can help somebody early, usually a cold won't be as bad and won't last as long.

Ian thought that he would probably return to the shipping operations until he received a management assignment. He thought he would be interested in being one of Santa's helpers on Christmas Eve, but knew that there was a lot of competition for these prestigious assignments. And he knew that to even be a candidate, you had to graduate in the top two percent of the CSS classes for the entire year. This was a major hurdle!

When everybody had had enough skiing and boarding, they met in the lodge for some of their favorite beverage – hot apple cider – before dinner. It was nice to relax after a hard day on the slopes. Everybody was busy chatting, and some were even doing a little flirting! Life was great! Teacher Marie looked around the room approvingly. "This has got to be the best group I've ever had together at one time!" she thought.

After awhile, dinner was served and it was delicious! Then came some music and some of their favorite elf songs. They all joined in with lots of energy, some of them as if they were opera singers! And of course, there was a lot of laughing and joking. Then the music slowed down and became soft and the lights were turned down a bit. Some of the elves started to dance.

"Ian, aren't you going to ask me to dance?" Elise whispered.

"Uh, yes, I was, like, uh," Ian stuttered. ("Arghh, I hate it when I talk this way," Ian said to himself. Calm down boy!")

"Would you like to dance, Elise?" Ian asked, this time with more confidence.

"I'd love to," she whispered and they soon found themselves out on the dance floor with the others. They danced as if they had been partners for a long, long time. This was a night to remember.

Chapter 18

Ian woke up early the following morning and decided to sit down for a few minutes and do some personal planning. He was half-way through the CSS training and felt good about his progress. He had completed all of the required speeches and found that public speaking was no longer a problem for him. Sure, he still got nervous before a speech, but he found out from Marie that this was normal. Even professional actors or singers get a little nervous before their performances. Made them do better according to Marie. Ian liked hearing this.

For the remaining five weeks, most of his time would be spent sharing research information with the others. These were usually in smaller groups, and compared to giving a speech to the whole class, it was really a piece of cake! During these small group sessions, Ian had gotten all of his remaining questions answered and soon found himself answering the questions of others. He liked being in this role.

Ian also needed to schedule a private meeting with Teacher

Marie. He hadn't given her his decision yet about being a manager. He was pretty sure that he'd like to be considered. Also, he wanted to talk to her about another assignment just in case he was not selected for a manager position. Taking this class had made Ian more comfortable around other elves. A job that would involve interaction with them was now appealing.

In shipping, you kind of worked on your own, although he certainly enjoyed being able to do research.

Finally, Ian had to decide on a graduation gift for Elise. This coming week was her final week.

Ian finished his "To Do" list and headed out the door to work. Today was going to be a slow day, so he'd have lots of time for research. He decided to assemble a personal list of little known facts about Christmas around the world. He had quite a few already from class. He would add some more research to them and then maybe select the top ten. He could use these whenever he was in a conversation with another elf and ran out of things to say. He laughed at the thought.

Ian's List

1 St. Nicholas was the child of wealthy parents. When they died, they left him a large inheritance. He decided to use his inheritance to help those less fortunate. This was the name of the early Santa Claus.

2 The first portrait of our present day Santa Claus was painted by Thomas Nast. He was inspired by Clement Moore's famous poem, "The Night Before Christmas"

3 Kris Kringle, another name for Santa, comes from the German word for Christ Child - "Christkindl"

4 There are 350 million Christians in Africa. On Christmas

Day, carols are sung from the Congo on down to South Africa. Meats are roasted, gifts are exchanged and family visits made.

5   A Buddhist thought: "Santa is actually very important to adults, teaching us unselfish, anonymous generosity."

6   A Muslim thought: "If it were not for the Christmas or Thanksgiving holidays, family relationships would not be as good as they are."

7   While Christmas Day is not a public holiday in China, Christmas decorations are now becoming more popular there. Santa is called Dun Che Lao Ren.

8   In Brazil, they create a nativity scene, or "presepio" which comes from the Hebrew word "presepium" or bed of straw, upon which the Baby Jesus first slept in Bethlehem.

9   Santa is called "Santa no ojisan" by children in Japan.   It means "Uncle Santa"

10   Gene Autry, famous American cowboy, recorded a song about Rudolph, the Red Nosed Reindeer in 1949.   It sold two million copies on its release and is still very popular to this day.

Ian finished work for the day and headed home. As he walked, he thought about Elise graduating. He would really miss her in class. In fact, he would really miss her all the time. He wanted to give her a gift, but couldn't think of a thing. He decided to give Samuel a call.

"Hey, Samuel, how's it going?" Ian asked.

"Oh, pretty good.   We're getting really busy," Samuel exclaimed. "But I like to stay busy so no problem. I haven't heard from you in awhile. I guess you've been busy with the CSS stuff, eh?"

"Yeah, I really have been, Samuel, but I'm moving along and the end is in sight!" Ian chuckled.

"Have you made your decision about whether you want to be a manager?" Samuel asked.

"I think I'm going to go for it, Samuel, but I haven't told anybody yet. You're the first. So keep it a secret, okay?"

"Don't worry, I won't tell a soul," Samuel said. "And congratulations on your decision. You're going to be a natural!"

"I sure hope you're right," Ian said with a laugh. "Hey, Samuel, another subject. You know that gal I was telling you about? Elise? Well, she's graduating this week and I want to give her a gift, but can't think of anything. Any thoughts?"

"Let me ask you something first," Samuel said. "Is she like a business associate, or is she more like a friend? Or maybe, a special friend?" Samuel asked with a definite smile in his voice.

"I consider her a special friend," Ian responded with a red face (but nobody could see it, thank goodness).

"Okay then, I would suggest you give her something personal. Girls always like jewelry. Give her a necklace or a locket with an inscription, or maybe a ring," Samuel said with another chuckle.

"Yeah, you're right about girls and jewelry," Ian said. "I'll have to give that some more thought. Thanks for your help, Samuel. Hey, we've got to go boarding again. Let me know when you have some time!"

"Will do, Ian. Talk to you soon, okay?" And they hung up.

Chapter 19

Ian decided to get a locket for Elise. He inscribed on the back "To Elise – You're the Best – Love, Ian". He hoped that she wouldn't be upset or offended by the word "Love". She could choose not to wear it, or whatever, but that's how he felt.

Elise's graduation ceremony was held in the conference room. It was a touching ceremony with nice background music. All the elves were dressed up and there were eighteen of them receiving diplomas. Santa and Mrs. Claus were the presenters. They both made short speeches. And so did Elise. She was chosen as the class valedictorian. That meant that Elise had the highest academic standing of the class!

Teacher Marie was the MC and got things going promptly. After a few preliminary remarks, she called on Mrs. Claus.

"Good evening, everyone!" Mrs. Claus began. "I'm so pleased to be with you all tonight. This is indeed a notable event. You have achieved so much and Santa and I have so much to be thankful for!" As she continued, you could hear the tears in her voice. It was so moving.

Next was Santa himself. "Ho, Ho, Ho, Hello my fellow elves!" he began. "Tonight is a milestone in your lives. You have worked very hard and you have achieved so much. You should be rightly proud of yourselves, as I am!"

After Santa came Elise. When she got to the podium, Ian was humbled by her radiance and beauty. And then she proceeded to give the most emotional and fulfilling valedictory ever! She was the best! The graduates gave her a standing ovation!

Following the presentation of diplomas, the graduates enjoyed a superb dinner thanks to Mrs. Claus. And then it was over.

Ian sat next to Elise, and as the graduates were starting to leave, Ian spoke in a low voice, "Elise, I have a little graduation present for you."

"Oh, Ian, you shouldn't have!" she said.

She opened the gift wrapping, and as she opened the box, her eyes glistened with small tears and she said, "Oh, Ian, it's beautiful!" As she read the inscription her mouth formed a smile. She then looked at Ian and said in a small voice, "Thank you, this is wonderful!"

Ian was speechless, but then started to smile and couldn't stop. What a great night!

The following Monday morning, Ian called Teacher Marie and they set up an appointment for that afternoon after work. The day went by very slowly for Ian. Finally, at five, Ian walked over for his meeting. Ms. Marie was waiting for him in her office.

"How did your day go, Ian?" she asked.

"It was another typical Monday, you know," Ian chuckled. "We got the load done, and we're in good shape, so I guess I shouldn't complain."

"Well, that's good," Teacher Marie said with a laugh. "Since you scheduled this meeting, how can I help you?".

"It's decision time," Ian began. "I've decided to go for a management position when there's one available. But, if this doesn't work out, I wanted to get some advice from you about what other non-management jobs might be available."

Teacher Marie stood up, with a big smile on her face, and shook Ian's hand very vigorously. "Congratulations on your decision, Ian!" she said. "I'm so happy! But let's not worry about what non-management jobs might be available. I can almost guarantee that you're going to get a management position!"

Ian was speechless as he shook Ms. Marie's hand and listened to her comments. A management job! He couldn't believe his ears!

Teacher Marie sat down and gave Ian a preview of what might lie ahead.

"The next few weeks will consist of more research and sharing," she began. "You'll also be reviewing, or cramming, if you will, for the final exam. The final exam score, as well as scores from the three formal speeches, plus scores from the informal presentations, will be compiled into an overall score. The elf with the highest overall score will be a candidate to accompany Santa on Christmas Eve. Actually, I should say the "elves" because there are two positions available on Christmas Eve."

She continued, "Now, the two elves that win this prestigious award will also be granted a special certificate which is called the "Christmas Eve With Santa" or "CEWS" Certificate. Having this certificate listed on your resume will virtually guarantee you any job you want!" she exclaimed.

This time it was Ian that stood up and held his hand out for a handshake with Ms.Marie. "Thank you so much for your words of support," Ian said. "I'm going to do my best to be a candidate!"

Sometimes when life gets confusing, you know
You have to hang in there and go with the flow

Are you going too fast? Are you going too slow?
You're not really sure. You just don't know.

But one thing you do know and this is for sure
If you give it your best shot, you'll always endure.

So hang in there, Elf, don't throw in the towel
Victory is coming, and soon you will yowl!

Chapter 20

The next three weeks were a blur. The research material presented by the elves at their meetings was really getting detailed and there seemed to be an endless supply. Half of their time in class was spent in presentations. The other half was used to review notes for the final exam. "Cramming," in other words.

Back on the job, the pace was starting to pick up as Christmas Eve approached. There was overtime everyday for Ian except, of course, on Wednesdays. After long days at work, he often found himself studying late into the night. "It's tough," Ian thought, "but worth it!" He kept telling himself that. {tenses} It made him feel better.

He didn't have any time to ski or play around on weekends. He thought of Elise often, but he knew she was very busy too with the year-end crunch. But, just about the time Ian was wondering if the long days would ever end, they did. It was "Week #10" of his CSS training. Tonight was his final exam!

When Ian arrived at the conference room, the other students were quietly entering the training room. There was no Mrs. Claus dinner tonight. They had been told to grab a bite before they came to class. There wasn't a lot of conversation, either. The elves went to their assigned seats.

Teacher Marie got their attention and started giving instructions while she handed out the exams. She told them that they could take as much time as needed up until ten o'clock. If they got done sooner, they could leave.

Ian looked at the exam. There were eighty True-False and Multiple Choice questions. This was followed by twenty essay questions. Ian knew that the essay answers would take a long time. He got going on the first eighty questions and finished them in about an hour. The multiple choice questions were tricky. He wasn't sure about a lot of his choices.

The essay questions were not difficult to answer, but he had to worry about the way he would format his answers. He knew that he would be graded as much on the format as on the content. This was critical so he took his time and gave a lot of thought to each answer. When he finally finished, he looked at the clock. It was 9:30 and at least half of the elves had already finished and left. He turned in his test to the teacher and headed home. As he walked along, he had a feeling of relief; there would be no more classes! When he got home, he was too excited to go to sleep, so he called Elise.

"Hi Elise," Ian said. "I hope I didn't wake you!"

"No, Ian," she said. "I just got home from work."

"Oh, good!" said Ian. "I just got home too. You know, we had finals tonight and I'm too wound up to go to sleep. I can't believe I'm finally done! No more classes!" he exclaimed.

"That's great, Ian!" Elise said. "I know how you feel! And Friday is graduation, right? Then we'll just have to wait and see what happens. You know, what the next step is, whether it's a new job or what."

"Yeah, I know," Ian said. They're going to announce the "CEWS" winners next week. I wonder who will be the lucky ones?" he asked.

"I have absolutely no clue," Elise said. "They have to select from a whole year's worth of candidates! There's so much competition. But, you know, I'm not going to worry about it. Like the saying goes, Just go with the flow! They laughed at that old elf motto, chatted a little longer, then said good night and hung up.

Ian went to work the next morning and lost himself in his work. It was really getting busy as they got closer and closer to Christmas Eve. Toward the end of the day, he got a phone call from Teacher Marie.

"Can you drop by my office at 6:00 tonight?" she asked in a solemn tone.

"I'll be there," Ian said quietly. "Is there a problem?"

"No, I just wanted to talk to you."

As Ian walked to Marie's office, he started to wonder what was up. Did he fowl up his exam? Maybe he should have checked it again instead of leaving at 9:30. He shouldn't have rushed the way he did. He knocked on Teacher Marie's office door.

She opened the door. "Hello, Ian," she said. "Come in, sit down," she motioned to the corner table and chairs.

Ian sat down quietly and started to get a funny feeling in his stomach.

Teacher Marie walked over and sat down across from him. She opened her test binder, looked down and then looked up slowly at Ian.

"Never, in my career as a teacher, has this ever happened," she said with her head still down. Then raising it slowly, she added, "but today it has. Ian, you scored 100 on your exam!" She broke into a big grin.

Ian couldn't believe his ears. Was this really happening? He broke into a big smile too, then got up and gave Marie a big hug. "I couldn't have done it without you!" he exclaimed.

They both sat down again, still smiling.

"Ian," Ms. Marie said. "One more thing. You and Elise have been selected to accompany Santa on Christmas Eve! It's official! You're to report to Santa tomorrow morning at 9:00 o'clock. He will give you a briefing on what needs to be done in the next few days before you take off. Also," Marie continued, "There'll be an official awards ceremony where you and Elise will receive the CEWS certificates, but it'll be after you return. That way, all the elves will be able to attend. They can't now because they're so busy. Plus, you'll be able to tell them about your trip. Sound Good?"

"Sounds too good to be true!" exclaimed Ian. "Thanks so much for everything!"

Chapter 21

The excitement was almost overwhelming for Ian. When he got back to his room there were several calls on his answering machine. Samuel and Kai and a bunch of other guys called to congratulate him. He decided he would call them later. But right now, Elise.

"Hi, Elise," he said when she answered. "Congratulations, partner!"

"Oh, Ian, this is so exciting!" she said. "I can't believe it's happening! And now we've got a meeting with Santa tomorrow, and in a few days, we'll be on our way! Aren't you excited too?" she asked.

"Very much so," he said. "I'm really looking forward to meeting with Santa, too. You know, we've all been on a kind of first name basis with him, but now it's really going to become a close relationship. Not only with him, but with Mrs. Claus as well."

"She's great to work with," Elise said. "You'll really like her. I know I do. They're a great couple!"

"Elise, do you want to get some breakfast tomorrow morning before we meet Santa?" Ian asked.

"Sounds good," she answered. "How about 8:00 in the cafeteria?"

"Okay. See you then," he said and they hung up.

Ian stayed up well into the night. He was just too excited to sleep. Plus, he was on the phone talking to his friends for a long, long time.

The next morning, he and Elise met for breakfast. She had been up late, as well. They were both very excited and couldn't eat much, but they sure had plenty to talk about Christmas Eve, new jobs, plans for the future, all the work to be done in the next few days, flying around the world, all at night, and more. Before they knew it, they were knocking on Santa's door.

"Ho, Ho, Ho," Santa chuckled when he opened the door. "Elise and Ian, my dear elves, welcome! Please come in!"

Santa's office looked like what a child's idea of heaven might be. It was full of toys, dolls, cars, games, and candy canes. Santa had a big desk with a big fat chair and he sat there with a big ledger that he used to keep track of everything.

"Sit down," he said. "I'll be right back. I'm going to go get the Mrs. Ho, Ho, Ho!"

They both returned in a moment. Mrs. Claus smiled and said, "Oh, my dears, I'm so happy for you. And Santa and I are so pleased to have your assistance!" She looked around the room at all the toys scattered all over the place, then looked at Santa.

"Dear," she said. "Maybe we could go to the dining room for our meeting? We'll have a bit more room and maybe have some refreshments as well?"

At this, Santa's eyes lit up, he laughed and said, "Great idea, my dear. Let's do it!"

As soon as they were settled in the dining room, in came an elf with some tea and fresh baked cookies. They looked wonderful and Santa quickly passed them around and took a few for himself. Mrs. Claus looked on with a knowing smile on her face. After a few minutes, Santa started the meeting.

"Okay," he began with his typical chuckle. "We've got three more days 'til Christmas Eve, my favorite time of the year! We've got to get the reindeer ready, get the sleigh packed, get some food prepared, and then make sure our "Naughty and Nice" list is in good shape."

"You two will be spending some time in each of those areas," he continued, "and there will be different elves to show you around, tell you what needs to be done, and answer your questions. Do you have any questions for me or Mrs. Claus?" he asked.

"Yes sir, I do," said Ian. "How long will we be gone?" he asked.

"We'll be gone about twenty-four hours," Santa responded

"Where will we go first?" Elise asked.

"We'll be in eastern Asia and New Zealand and lots of Pacific Island countries first," Santa said, "and then we'll continue west while we zigzag up and down."

"And what will be last?' Elise asked again

"Oh, let's see, Ho, Ho, Ho, Santa responded. "That would probably be Hawaii which is very close to where we started!"

"So we'll actually be part of a twenty-four hour long Christmas Eve around the world, won't we?" Ian asked.

"Yes indeed!" Santa said with a big smile.

"And that's why we need to make certain that you and the reindeer have plenty to eat while you're gone," Mrs. Claus beamed.

"What kind of food will the reindeer have?" Elise asked.

"Oh, they love oats!" Mrs. Claus said. "I make up a special recipe of oats and sugar. I add some milk and butter and then bake them into little pellets. It's their special treat of the year. Makes them fly faster, too! You and Ian will find yourselves being very well loved by the reindeer by the time you return home again!" she laughed.

"What will Santa and the two of us have to eat?" Ian asked.

"Oh, Santa will have plenty to eat while he makes his deliveries!" They all laughed at that one.

"As for you and Elise, I'm not going to tell you what it is. I want to surprise you!" she laughed. "But I will tell you this. It's portable!"

Santa asked if there were any more questions. There weren't, so he took them to the barn to meet the reindeer. It was lunchtime for them and Elise and Ian would be their "servers" today.

They followed Santa over to his barn. It was a typical barn with individual stalls for the nine reindeer. They heard the reindeer making guttural type sounds as they walked in. They seemed to know what was coming.

Santa showed Ian and Elise where the hay was and how much to give them. At first, they fed them by hand so that the reindeer could get to know them and then they gave each a couple of pitch forks full of hay for them to chew on later. They also gave each an apple for a treat and made sure there was plenty of water for them to drink.

"During our flight on Christmas Eve, we don't have to bring much water because the reindeer like to eat snow," Santa said.

"The reindeer seemed to like you," Santa said when they were done. "By the time we take off, you'll be best friends! Ho, Ho, Ho," he laughed. "By the way, you need to give them their food three times a day while we're still here on the ground, but when we get underway on Christmas Eve, they'll let you know when it's time!" he laughed.

"Okay, Elise, why don't you go join Mrs. Claus for awhile," Santa said. "She'll show you what needs to be packed, you know, the food and stuff for you guys and the oats for the reindeer. I'll go over the list of presents with Ian and we'll start packing! All right, let's get it on. Ho, Ho, Ho!"

The next days went by very rapidly. Santa and Mrs. Claus were wonderful to work with. So loving and caring. All of the helpers in their house loved them. So did the reindeer.

Ian and Elise loved the reindeer, too. They spent a great deal of their time feeding them, talking to them, and kind of just hanging around with them. The reindeer loved the extra attention. They showed their gratitude by licking their hands when they gave them their apples. It was fun.

On the final day before takeoff that night, the reindeer sensed that it was almost time and started getting excited. Ian and Elise went around and gave them a little extra treat which helped calm them down.

"We'll be coming back to hitch you up in a little while," Ian said as he and Elise started to leave. Just then, they heard a loud sneeze which they'd never heard before.

"What the...? What was that?" Elise stammered. "It sounded like it was coming from Rudolph's stall!" They ran over.

"Well, his nose is kind of wet but sometimes it gets that way when he eats apples," Ian said. "Let's go check the others."

They went around to each stall. Dasher looked okay. So did Dancer, Prancer and Vixen. Comet was fine. Cupid was dozing. So were Donner and Blitzen. They all looked okay and their noses were dry. They checked Rudolph again. Yep, his nose was still wet and while they were standing there, Rudolph sneezed again.

"We better tell Santa," they agreed and ran over to his office.

"Aw, that Rudolph and his nose are always a little different from the others. I don't think there's anything to worry about," Santa declared. "Why don't you elves go take a little nap before we take off. I'll see you over here around 6:00 for dinner and then we'll be heading out," he added with a big smile.

Chapter 22

Ian and Elise now had rooms in Santa's house and they really enjoyed their stay there even though they were working many hours each day. But they weren't the only ones. Everybody there was busy getting ready for Christmas Eve. There were about twenty elves that worked directly for Santa or Mrs. Claus. They all had a chance to get together during breaks or during their meals. It was fun to get to know everybody.

Some of the elves were kind of like cabinet members. They had a lot of authority over all of the operations at the North Pole. Santa really relied on their expertise and guidance. Many of them had been there for a long, long time. They were nice people, but sometimes Ian and Elise would have conversations on the side about how old fashioned they were in many ways. They often wondered if there weren't better ways to carry out some of the operations. Oh well, they decided, it's not something to worry about at this time.

Everybody got together for a really nice Christmas Eve dinner and then it was time to go! The reindeer were hitched up, Rudolph's nose was still wet, but he seemed okay, the sleigh was loaded with presents, they had their own meals, (Mrs. Claus made them like the ones soldiers got, known as MRE's or "Meals, ready to eat"), and oats for the reindeer. Santa had his list and a big smile on his face when he yelled, "Ho, Ho, Ho, Merry Christmas!" Hearing this, the reindeer lunged forward and they quickly took off. Santa circled the North Pole so they could wave goodbye to everybody, (there were hundreds of elves on the ground waving and yelling!), and then they were off.

Once they got into the air, they went amazingly fast! Santa was seated in the middle of the front seat with Ian and Elise on either side. Santa had on his favorite Christmas outfit and Ian and Elise had matching red outfits which were very warm. They also brought along extra jackets and backpacks. It was exciting to sit up there and fly around the world.

They soon reached their first stop and glided to a stop on the roof. While Santa went down the chimney, Ian and Elise checked the reindeer. They weren't too hungry yet, but it wouldn't be long before they would be. Elise heard Rudolph sneeze a couple of times, and in the dark night, it made his nose kind of flicker. She mentioned it to Ian and they agreed to keep their eyes open. Fortunately, the night was clear.

It was amazing to watch Santa maneuver the sleigh. His instincts were awesome! He knew just when to make turns and when to rise up or head down. The reindeer were very responsive to his little tugs on the reins. Ian didn't know how Santa did it, but then reminded himself that he had done this so many, many times over the years.

They continued on schedule over Asia, including India, China, and Russia, then on to Europe, down through the Holy Land, and then down into Africa. From there they would hop over to South America, then continue up through Central America, Mexico, and then to their biggest stop of all; the United States. Before leaving Africa, Ian checked Rudolph. He was sneezing a lot more and his nose didn't look too good. However, all the other reindeer were fine. They were enjoying the extra attention they were getting.

Ian told Santa about Rudolph's sneezing, but Santa shrugged and said, "Don't worry, my boy, Rudolph is one strong little reindeer. He'll be okay."

They left Africa and headed for the southern tip of South America. While crossing the Atlantic, they noticed what appeared to be a build-up of dense clouds beneath them. However, it was clear above the clouds, where they were, so they continued across the ocean to Argentina and continued their deliveries.

They worked their way up the continent, visiting many countries. When they were done with Colombia and Venezuela, they headed up through the Caribbean Islands, straight up to Newfoundland, Canada. It was quite a bit colder, Ian thought. As they got into the northern part of the US, the clouds that they had been traveling under started to settle lower and turn into a fog. Pretty soon it got really thick and Santa had to depend on Rudolph's red nose to guide him. Rudolph was happy to help out. After all, this is why he was part of the team, wasn't it?

They maneuvered their way through the fog okay, but every once in awhile, Rudolph would sneeze, and the light would flicker. Santa could manage okay though, so no problem. They continued onward, heading west. About the time they were around the Denver area, when Ian and Elise were feeding the reindeer, they discovered that Rudolph really looked bad. He was plugged up and he was sneezing like crazy. He wouldn't even eat the treats they brought him. His nose was flickering quite a bit with the constant sneezing and, all of a sudden, with a big sneeze, it went completely out!

They were in the dark and in the fog, to boot! When Santa crawled out of the chimney and saw how dark it was, his mouth dropped, and for the first time ever, Ian and Elise saw Santa without a smile on his face!

"What's wrong with Rudolph?" Santa asked. "How come his nose isn't shining? We can't do anything in this fog without some light!"

"Santa," Ian said. "Rudolph has a bad cold and it has him really plugged up! Elise has some cold medicine in her first aid pouch. I'm sure it'll help him. Plus, she's a very good nurse. She'll get him on his feet real soon and we can get his light on and get going again!"

"That's good to hear," said Santa. "How long before we can get underway?"

"It says on the bottle that it doesn't even become effective for an hour, possibly two!" Elise exclaimed. "Plus, the patient needs to lie down and keep warm while the medicine is being taken. Santa, we should put Rudolph in the back of the sleigh!"

"Oh, my goodness!" Santa exclaimed. "Yes, let's put Rudolph in back and get him covered up! But we can't stop! We'll get behind and the children who get up early won't have anything in their stockings or under the tree!"

While Santa and Elise were moving Rudolph, Ian went to his backpack and took out his cell phone. He had ordered it a few weeks ago when he was doing his research on navigation and it was equipped with GPS. He had read the users' manual and had played around with it, so he knew how to operate it. "But will it be detailed enough for Santa's needs?" he wondered. "On the other hand, what choice did they have?"

"Santa," he said, "I have an idea. Do you remember Teacher Marie talking to you about GPS a few weeks ago?"

"Yes, my boy, I do but I told her that it wouldn't be necessary. That we were able to get around fine without it. I like to do things the old-fashioned way, I guess."

"I know, Santa," Ian said. There's nothing wrong with that. But right now we've got an emergency. I think this thing will help us out while Rudolph is healing. Isn't it worth a try?"

Santa took his cap off and scratched his head for a moment.

"Ian," he said, "I think you're our only hope. Let's do it!"

"Thanks, Santa! I'll give it my best shot! You said we're in the Denver area, right?" Ian asked.

"That's right son. We are. In fact, I'm pretty sure we're in a suburb called Longmont. What does your GPS thing say?"

"It has confirmed Longmont! Are you ready to take off?" Ian yelled so that Elise could hear in back. "I'll stay up here next to you, Santa, so you can hear the directions, okay?"

"Ho, Ho, Ho, Merry Christmas!" yelled Santa. This was his favorite command to get the reindeer underway.

Ian and his GPS worked like magic. The fog was still thick, but it wasn't all the way to the ground, so while they were in the different towns, Santa could easily make his way from rooftop to rooftop. However, when they had to climb to high altitudes to make good time, Santa had a problem. The clouds were thick and hard to navigate. This is when the GPS really came in handy. Before long, they had made up the time that was lost while they were caring for Rudolph and trying to figure out what to do. Santa's smile had returned and it was bigger than ever!

They were about an hour from home when they heard some rustling sounds from the back. Rudolph was standing up with a big smile on his face and his nose was shining brightly! He was raring to go again! Elise was smiling too, but Ian detected some tears of joy in her eyes. They hitched Rudolph back up and you could tell he was happy. His nose was brighter than ever! And all of the other reindeer still loved him as they shouted out with glee!

When they came in for a landing at home, Mrs. Claus and all of the elves turned out to welcome them back. They had heard of the near disaster and how Ian had saved the night and how Elise had saved Rudolph! They gave them a grand ovation! Santa leaned over and whispered under his breath to them, "I have some new jobs I'd like to talk to you two about!"

CPSIA information can be obtained at www.ICGtesting.com
Printed in the USA
BVOW03s1035300913

332470BV00002B/5/P